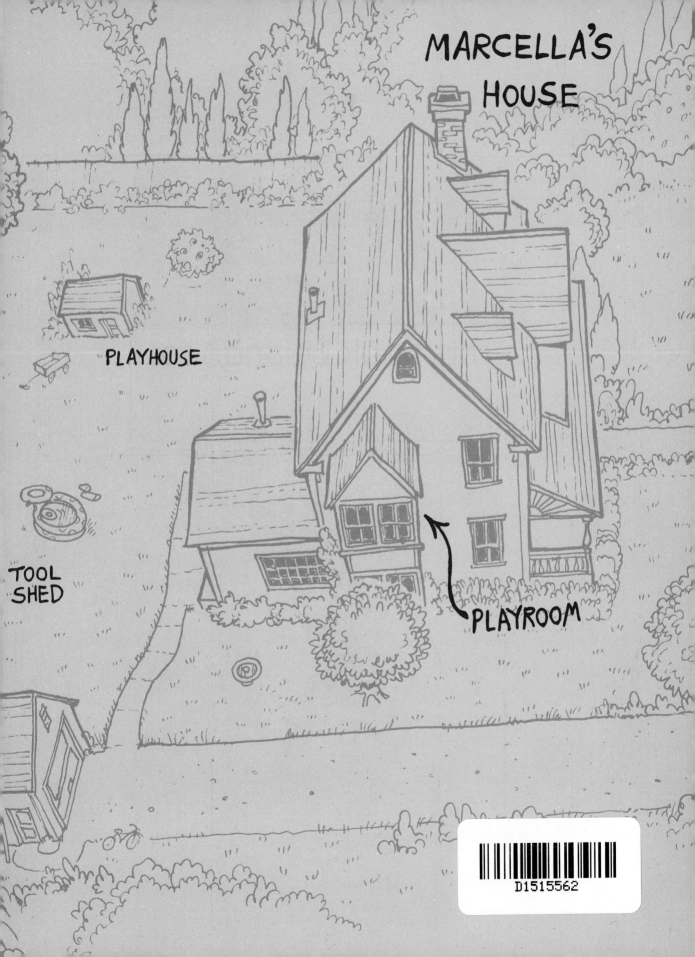

This book belongs to:

Kellie Kunkel

Raggedy Ann & Andy's

GROW AND LEARN LIBRARY

VOLUME 16

THE SLEEPOVER

™
A LYNX BOOK

This book is published by Lynx Books, a division of Lynx Communications, Inc., 41 Madison Avenue, New York, New York 10010. The name "Lynx" together with the logotype consisting of a stylized head of a lynx is a trademark of Lynx Communications, Inc.

Raggedy Ann and Andy's Grow-and-Learn Library, the names and depictions of Raggedy Ann, Raggedy Andy and all related characters are trademarks of Macmillan, Inc.

Marcella was very happy because she was about to visit her good friend Kathryn. She was going to take one of her dolls along! The dolls listened eagerly as Marcella told them all about the plans she and Kathryn had made. Each of them secretly hoped he or she would be the one Marcella would choose to take for the visit.

"Would you like to come, Sunny Bunny?" Marcella asked. Sunny Bunny was delighted!

"I'm going to pack my overnight bag now, and then I'll come right back for you," Marcella called as she ran out of the room.

"Overnight bag?" Sunny Bunny said to himself.

"Did Marcella say 'overnight bag'?" asked Sunny Bunny in a slightly worried voice. He had never slept over at anyone's house before, and he wasn't quite sure he liked the idea.

"She did," answered Babette the French Doll. "You're going to get to spend the whole night at Kathryn's house. You're very lucky, Sunny Bunny."

"I wish Marcella had picked me," Tim the Toy Soldier sighed wistfully.

"Me, too," said The Camel with the Wrinkled Knees.

Raggedy Ann could see that Sunny Bunny was feeling a little shy about going. "I once went with Marcella to Kathryn's house and spent the whole night," she told him. "All the dolls there are very nice. You will have a good time, Sunny Bunny."

Before they could say another word, they heard Marcella running across the hall.

In a flash, Marcella rushed in and scooped up Sunny Bunny. Then she skipped out the door with him in one arm and her little suitcase in the other.

Sunny Bunny looked back. He already missed his friends' smiling faces and the playroom he was leaving behind.

When they arrived at Kathryn's house, the two girls were very happy to see each other. They hugged so tightly that Sunny Bunny got just a little bit crushed! Then the two girls raced up to Kathryn's playroom. Kathryn wanted to show Marcella one of her newest games.

While Marcella and Kathryn played together, Sunny Bunny had a chance to look around.

"It is a very nice playroom, and Kathryn's dolls do look friendly," he admitted to himself. "But they don't look like my friends at home," he thought with an inward sigh. And all day long, while Marcella and Kathryn played, Sunny Bunny thought about how much he missed his friends and how he longed to be back in his own playroom again.

Soon it was bedtime. Marcella kissed Sunny Bunny
good night. Then she and Kathryn went to bed.
When the dolls were quite sure that the girls were
asleep for the night, they slipped down from their shelves
and introduced themselves.

"Hi, Sunny Bunny," said lots of friendly voices.

"I'm Rosa from Spain," said a pretty doll with a kind voice.

"And we are Henry and Clara. We are twins," said two little Dutch dolls.

"Hi there, partner, I'm Tex," said a cowboy doll. "This here is Clarence, my trusty pony," he added.

"I'm Mary, and this is Tiny," said a pretty china doll shyly. Sunny Bunny smiled at Mary and her little lamb.

"Welcome to our playroom," said a little voice that was hopping right by.

"That is Joey," Rosa explained. "Joey is a baby kangaroo. He loves to hop all over the place when Kathryn isn't around."

Even though all of the dolls were very nice, Sunny Bunny still missed his own friends and his own playroom. Henry and Clara made him think of Greta the Dutch Doll. Clarence made him homesick for Tallyho the Wooden Horse. And Tiny made him miss his old friend Sam Lamb more than ever.

"Is something wrong?" Rosa asked him.

"I've never slept away from home before," he told her in a very soft voice.

"Oh, I see," Rosa said kindly. She thought for a moment. Then she had an idea.

"Why don't we all play a game?" Rosa suggested.
"Then Sunny Bunny won't think about being homesick so
much. Would you like that?" she asked him cheerfully.

"Well, yes . . . it might be nice to play a game," he said slowly. "We always have fun when we play games at home," Sunny Bunny added hopefully.

"Great. Let's play London Bridge," sang out Henry and Clara.

"I think I'll just watch," said Sunny Bunny. He had never played London Bridge before, so he was afraid that he wouldn't know what to do.

All the dolls lined up in two rows, and Henry and Clara made the "bridge." Everyone seemed to be having lots of fun.

It was Mary who noticed that Sunny Bunny looked
even sadder than before. "Don't you like to play London
Bridge?" she asked.

"I don't know," he answered. "I've never played it
before."

"Then why don't you pick a game *you'd* like to play," suggested Tex.

Sunny Bunny asked if they could play his favorite game, leapfrog. The other dolls had never played leapfrog, so Rosa asked Sunny Bunny if he would show them what to do.

In no time, the dolls were laughing and playing. Joey liked the game most of all. Sunny Bunny and Joey could jump farther than anyone else. Joey could even jump over several dolls at the same time!

After the game was over, the dolls were out of breath.
"That was fun," said Henry and Clara.
"We're so glad you came to visit, Sunny Bunny," said Rosa.

For a moment, Sunny Bunny felt shy again. Then he thought about how nice the other dolls were when he was teaching them how to play his favorite game.

"Would you show me how to play one of *your* games?" asked Sunny Bunny. "Then I can show the dolls in my playroom how to play it when I go home."

The dolls were very happy and showed him how to play duck-duck goose.

Next Sunny Bunny taught the dolls how to play hide-and-seek.

"Close your eyes and count to ten, Rosa," said Sunny Bunny. "Be sure not to peek," he added.

He helped the other dolls find places to hide so Rosa could look for them.

The dolls loved Sunny Bunny's game. They all laughed when Rosa found where they were hiding. And they all clapped when Sunny Bunny ran "home" and called out, "Home free all!"

"What a wonderful game," Mary said. "I would love to visit your playroom, Sunny Bunny."

Sunny Bunny thought about how much fun they would all have if Kathryn brought some of her dolls to sleep over in Marcella's playroom one day.

After playing so many games, the dolls were very tired. One by one, they curled up and went to sleep. Sunny Bunny didn't feel like a stranger anymore, and he wasn't homesick at all.

"It isn't so bad sleeping away from home after all," he thought to himself, snuggling up into a furry ball.

The next day, when it was time for Marcella to go home, Sunny Bunny said good-bye to all his new friends. As much as he wanted to return to his own playroom again, he knew he would miss the new friends he had made.

When he was back at home, Sunny Bunny told the playroom dolls all about his adventure. Then he taught them how to play London Bridge and duck-duck goose. His friends in the playroom were very impressed!

"It was fun sleeping over at Kathryn's," Sunny Bunny had to admit.

"You mean you weren't homesick?" asked Babette.

"Oh, I was—just a bit," Sunny Bunny said with a little sigh. "But now that I know what it's like, I won't be next time," he replied. And, from the corner of his eye, he saw Raggedy Ann smile proudly at him.